What's Next?

by Lisa Thompson
illustrated by Lisa Thompson and
Matthew Stapleton

PICTURE WINDOW BOOKS
Minneapolis, Minnesota

Editor: Jacqueline A. Wolfe
Managing Editor: Catherine Neitge
Story Consultant: Terry Flaherty
Page Production: Melissa Kes/ James Mackey
Creative Director: Keith Griffin
Editorial Director: Carol Jones

First American edition published in 2006 by
Picture Window Books
5115 Excelsior Boulevard
Suite 232
Minneapolis, MN 55416
1-877-845-8392
www.picturewindowbooks.com

First published in Australia in 2004 by
Blake Publishing Pty Ltd
ABN 50 074 266 023
108 Main Rd
Clayton South VIC 3168

Printed in the United States of America.

Library of Congress Catalog-in-Publication Data
Thompson, Lisa, 1969-
What's next? / by Lisa Thompson ; illustrated by Lisa Thompson and Matthew Stapleton.— 1st American ed.
p. cm. — (Read-it! chapter books) (Wonder wits)
Summary: Luke and Sophie are chosen to visit Future Industries to stay overnight in the Tomorrow Lab where some futuristic inventions are being tested.
ISBN 1-4048-1350-0 (hardcover)
[1. Inventions—Fiction.] I. Stapleton, Matthew, ill. II. Title. III. Series.
PZ7.T371634Wha 2005
[Fic]—dc22

2005009829

Table of Contents

Thinking Caps 4
The Futurist 16
The Great
Visionary Hall 26
The Tomorrow Lab 30
Imagining the Future . . 40

More Stuff

Future Predictions 44
Great Visionaries 46
Areas to Watch 47

Chapter 1
Thinking Caps

Luke was puzzled. All day, he'd had this strange feeling that he couldn't shake.

"This is going to sound weird, Sophie," he confided to his best friend, "but I feel like someone or something is reading my thoughts."

Sophie stopped gluing a piece of fiberglass to a half-finished invention. Her look told Luke something was up.

Luke had a

“Soph, what’s going on?” Luke asked.

“Don’t panic or you’ll wreck our chance!” Sophie instructed. “No one is reading your thoughts. You’re just being tracked. We both are.”

“What do you mean? Who’s tracking us?” Luke asked, as he paced the work shed. “And what chance could I wreck?”

Sophie took the cap she’d given to Luke that morning from his head. She took her cap off as well and pointed to the tiny dots inside and said, “These tiny dots are brain wave trackers.”

strange feeling.

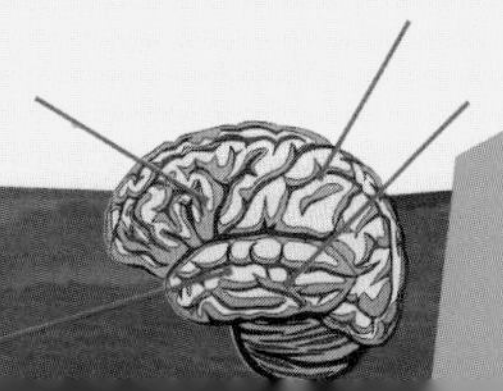

"The dots read your brain waves while you wear the hat," said Sophie. "When the brain waves are at the right frequency, the dots download information into your brain. They're still in the testing stage, but these caps are one version of a homework tool that inventors at Future Industries have been working on. They're real thinking caps! Imagine, no more long hours of homework."

Sophie hid the cap behind her back and continued, "That's why I didn't tell you. I knew you would be pulling the cap apart in seconds, trying to see how it works."

"What inventor wouldn't?" Luke asked, trying to grab the cap.

"Inventors who want to get chosen by Future Industries to spend a night in their Tomorrow Lab. Inventors who want to present the team with their own ideas for the future," said Sophie. "Inventors who can be trusted not to pull inventions apart."

"You're kidding!" said Luke, letting out a whistle. "You mean THE Tomorrow Lab? The one we have been trying to get into—forever?"

Sophie smiled. "Wearing these caps today is a test to see if we can be trusted with their inventions," she explained as she held out the cap. "Now whatever you do, don't wreck it."

Just then, a delivery man knocked on the door and said, "I have a pick up and special delivery from Future Industries for Luke and Sophie."

“That’s us,” said Sophie, signing for a small box. Opening it, she found a screen the size of a trading card. Sophie touched the screen, and a bald man appeared on the screen. Luke and Sophie recognized him from photographs. He was Dr. Seevers, the head inventor of Future Industries.

“Hello, Luke and Sophie,” he beamed. “These are our wallet smart cards. We’re still working on increasing the memory time but they’re good, huh? Hold the screen up so I can look at your work space.”

see possible future inventions.

Sophie scanned the card around the room.

"Looks like you've got some interesting inventions of your own," said Dr. Seevers.

"So, do we get to hang out in the lab?" blurted Luke excitedly.

"Luke!" gasped Sophie.

"Actually, yes! We'd like you to spend tonight in the Tomorrow Lab if that's OK with you."

"Absolutely!" said Sophie.

"That's more than OK with me!" Luke said.

What do you think the world will

"Good," responded the doctor. "Now place the thinking caps and this card in the box, so the delivery man can return them to our secret laboratories. There is a vehicle waiting at the front of your work shed to transport you to our headquarters. Don't worry about bringing anything. Everything you need is waiting for you in the Tomorrow Lab." The card started to beep. "We're out of time. I'll see you in the not-too-distant future!"

be like in 10 ... 20 ... 100 years?

Before Luke and Sophie had the chance to say anything else, the screen went blank. They gave the caps and card to the delivery man and walked outside.

They had never seen a car like this before. It had three wheels and hugged the road. On the front of the car were solar panels. A door slid open to reveal the interior.

"Hello. I am a Future Industries transportation pod," said a voice from the dashboard.

What inventions would you

"Where's the driver?" asked Luke, as he and Sophie climbed into the pod.

The dash spoke again, "I am a pre-programmed vehicle run by electricity and solar power. I am designed to take you to your destination by the most efficient route and in the shortest time possible. Tests show me to be 95 percent safer than a human-driven vehicle. If you sit back, I will activate your restraints."

like to see in the future?

Seat belts automatically slid across Luke and Sophie, and the pod door closed. Sophie pressed a button, thinking it would lower the window. But a beach scene appeared instead.

"Oops," said Sophie. "I just wanted to put the window down."

"You can put the window down and have normal view," replied the dash. "Or I have a range of UV-protected scenes like this that can be viewed instead."

Design your own transportation pod. What

“Normal view will be fine,” giggled Sophie. She felt silly talking to a car dash.

“Say when,” said the dash, as the window lowered.

“When,” said Luke, who had just found a small screen with controls to play games. “This pod is so cool.”

“Thank you,” the dash responded. The pod engine started. Sophie and Luke felt the pod lift and hover above the road.

“Look out, future, here we come,” whispered Luke nervously, as the pod sped away.

kind of special features would it have?

Chapter 2
The Futurist

Dr. Seevers greeted Luke and Sophie at the entrance to Future Industries headquarters. He said,"I'm meeting you here because entry into the building is possible only after an iris scan."

He directed them to look into a small camera. "This camera will record the patterns in your eyes. They will be downloaded to the building's main computer system and allow you to move around the building."

In the future, banks may install iris

They followed him through a maze of corridors. Dr. Seevers noticed that Luke and Sophie were jogging to keep up with him.

"Sorry," he chuckled and slowed down. "I forgot I'm wearing a pair of our latest spring-bound joggers. They increase average walking speed by up to 50 percent. We think they will be perfect for helping people exercise more because it will take them less time to get places."

scans in automatic teller machines.

"They're very clever," said Sophie, admiring the shoes.

"Actually the idea came from my team of futurists after one of their trend-finding sessions," said Dr. Seevers.

"What's a futurist trend-finding session?" asked Luke.

"I think the best person to explain is my head futurist. She is scheduled to meet you here any minute. I must go and prepare things in the Tomorrow Lab," Dr. Seevers said.

Flow charts, pie charts, diagrams,

As Dr. Seevers left them, a wall slid open on the other side of the room. It revealed a woman sitting at a large, round table, surrounded by giant monitors. She eyed them over thin, rectangular glasses.

"Welcome to the Future Industries trend tank," she smiled. "I'm Ms. Fullbright."

"You're the first futurist we've ever met," said Sophie, stepping into the room. She felt overwhelmed by the data and diagrams flickering on the giant screens.

and data ... data ... data!

Luke's eyes were glued to the streams of changing information. He asked, "What does a futurist do? And how do you help invent things?"

"Let me show you," said Ms. Fullbright, pointing to the main monitor. "A futurist tries to predict what the future will be like by looking at what is going on in the world today. We find patterns that occur in different countries. By gathering this information, we try to predict what kinds of inventions will be needed in the future."

Futurists try to predict what the future may be like by

“What kind of information do you look at?” asked Sophie.

“Pretty much everything,” said Ms. Fullbright, scrolling through pictures and charts on the screen. “How people live, think, and behave. How they want to live and population changes. Fashions and fads, what is happening in the environment, and world events. After we gather the information, we find patterns by a kind of dot-to-dot process.”

looking at today's data and patterns from the past.

“How does that work?” asked Sophie, taking a seat.

“Well, let's look at the spring-bound joggers. You saw the ones Dr. Seevers was wearing?” Ms. Fullbright asked.

Sophie and Luke nodded.

“That idea came about after my team found that people wanted to be healthier and exercise more, but didn’t feel they had enough time. Many people didn’t even walk short distances, as they found walking too slow.”

Spring-bound joggers let you

Ms. Fullbright continued, "So we identified the trend of people wanting to walk, but thinking that walking was too slow to use as a regular method of transportation. Then we thought, what if there was a shoe that got people where they wanted to go in less time? That way, they could use the shoe for both transportation and exercise. They would have a healthier lifestyle and save time."

walk from A to B faster!

"Do all the ideas at Future Industries come from looking at data and trends?" asked Sophie.

"No. This data is only a guide for what MIGHT happen, not what WILL happen. Our predictions are not always right. The future is a very unpredictable place. Who knows what's going to happen tomorrow!" Ms. Fullbright laughed.

Even with lots of data, the

"Some of the greatest inspiration for inventions doesn't come from studying data, but from observing truly amazing imaginations." Ms. Fullbright opened a door to a neon-lit corridor. "Come. I'll show you the Great Visionary Hall on our way to the Tomorrow Lab."

future is still unpredictable.

Chapter 3
The Great Visionary Hall

The ceiling of the Great Visionary Hall was like a long movie screen. It flickered with drawings, film stills, and sketches of future worlds.

There were robots of all shapes and sizes, floating cities, flying cars, colonies on the moon and in space, weather machines, sealed dome homes to live in, and time travel machines.

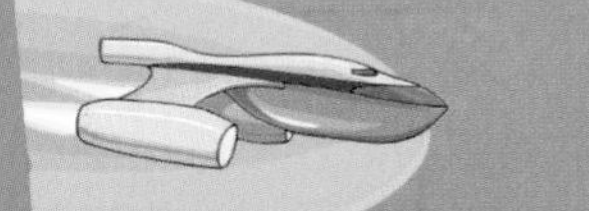

The ceiling flickered

"This is unreal!" gasped Luke.

Sophie nodded in agreement and said, "There is just so much here! Look at the shape of that future house." She pointed to a building that looked like a giant glass egg on its side.

with visions of the future.

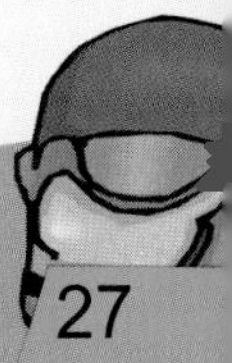

“These visions of the future came from filmmakers, artists, science-fiction writers, designers, and visionaries,” explained Ms. Fullbright. “These ideas aren’t always practical, but scientists and inventors are inspired to turn them into reality. Ideas need to inspire the imagination so deeply that people will work for decades, possibly a lifetime, to make them become real.”

Inventing the future takes

They reached the doors of the Tomorrow Lab. “This is where I leave you,” she smiled encouragingly. “We hope you like our vision of the future that is behind these doors. Maybe you will come away with your own ideas for the Great Visionary Hall. Have fun.”

vision and perseverance.

Chapter 4
The Tomorrow Lab

The door slid open, and Luke and Sophie stepped into the Tomorrow Lab. The lab looked like the interior of a house, but the furniture was very strange.

A holographic image of a boy and a girl appeared on one of the walls. They were about the same age as Luke and Sophie.

"Welcome. We are your holographic helpers," said the boy. "My name is Zac."

The Tomorrow Lab—the

"Another term for us is computer-generated companions," said the girl. "My name is Lulu."

"We are here to answer your questions," they said together. "Feel free to ask us anything."

Sophie saw a table covered in small gadgets. She picked up two small, foam-like shapes.

"You are holding ear-ins, Sophie. They fit into your ear and translate languages," explained Lulu.

“You use them with a holojector lesson helper. This allows you to do your homework with people from around the world.” Lulu said, her image now appeared on a screen mounted on the table. “This holojector is much more advanced than the computer screens you use now.”

“ I’ll bet!” said Sophie. She held up a wristband and asked, “What about this?”

A holojector lesson helper

Lulu explained, “It is a wrist set that does all kinds of computer tasks like Internet and e-mail. It is also a phone, camera, and video. And, of course, it can tell the time. Kids of the future will love them.”

“What’s that weird machine in the far corner?” asked Luke.

“That is a virtual reality trainer where you can practice sports like rock climbing or bungee jumping,” explained Zac.

lets you see people in 3-D.

Zac transferred himself to a monitor near the virtual reality trainer and said, "This will replace the home gym. It has full sensory capabilities. I am told you feel as if you are doing the real thing."

"Can we try it?" asked Luke.

"Yes. But before you do," said Lulu, "can I ask both of you to put on the smart clothes that have been laid out for you?"

Smart clothes—

Lulu explained, “These clothes will monitor your temperature and heart rate so we can keep you at maximum comfort while you are here.”

“They are also self-cleaning,” added Zac, “just like all the fabrics you see here. They are fitted with tiny nanorobots, invisible to the eye, that clean constantly.”

Luke and Sophie put on their smart clothes. Zac guided Luke on a mountain climb. Lulu and Sophie tried a bungee jump.

"That jump made me hungry," said Sophie. "Do you think I could get something to eat?"

"Of course," said Lulu. A wall slid back to reveal an eating station. There was chocolate cake, fresh fruit, and something else that looked somewhat familiar.

"They're vegetables!" said Luke, picking up an ear of red corn. "But they're the wrong colors."

"New varieties are produced all the time," said Zac, pointing to purple tomatoes.

"You should try the healthy chocolate cake," suggested Lulu. "It has the goodness of fruit and vegetables but still tastes like chocolate."

Next, Lulu showed Sophie and Luke the intelligent garbage can that sorted and recycled its own contents. They toured the virtual book library, and chatted to future friends from all over the world using ear-ins and the holojector. Zac showed them how to rearrange the walls of the room using a remote monitor.

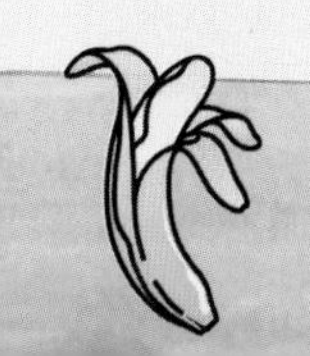

As they were getting ready for their night in the Tomorrow Lab, Sophie spotted a pair of glasses. “What do these do?”

“They are information download specs,” said Lulu. “You put them on, and they download information into your brain. They are also called thinking specs.”

Information download specs download

"Isn't there a thinking cap that does that?" asked Luke.

"Yes," Lulu answered. "The cap was an earlier model. It is very successful, but the specs are much faster."

"The future hasn't even happened, and it's already being updated," laughed Sophie.

"The future of the future," said Luke, trying on the specs. "What a very futuristic idea!"

information into your brain.

Chapter 5
Imagining the Future

The following morning, Dr. Seevers asked Luke and Sophie to present their ideas for the future. Inventors, scientists, and futurists gathered in the Great Visionary Hall.

The lights dimmed and the ceiling filled with sketches and drawings done by Sophie and Luke. They'd thought of ideas for housing, transportation, communication, environment, and medicine.

And, of course, there were lots of weird and wonderful gizmos!

Edible night passes, Eyemaxers, mat

Sophie and Luke had designed edible candy that made your body glow in the dark, round mat portals for instant transport between places, and something they called the Eyemaxer.

The Eyemaxer gave long-distance, night vision to the human eye. It also allowed the eye to zoom in and out and to take photographs.

But the invention that really grabbed the attention of the audience was a little patch that looked like a small, round Band-Aid. Luke and Sophie called it the cat-nap, memory restorer.

portals, and cat nap memory restorers.

Sophie explained its purpose, “In the future, more people are going to live longer. To stop memories from fading over time, you wear one of these while you sleep. It will restore people’s memories.”

“No excuse for forgetting things when you have one of these gizmos,” said Luke.

“Fascinating!” said Dr. Seevers. “I shall get my team on it right away—under your direction, of course. These ideas for the future are extremely inspiring. Do you have more?”

What invention would you

“Of course!” said Sophie. “We now know that the future is a lot closer than we thought. Actually, it’s only an imagination away.”

“And,” added Luke, “we figure that, even if the future doesn't turn out exactly as we plan, it’s still going to be a very exciting place. In fact, it’s the kind of world that lets you invent like crazy!”

like to see in the future?

Future

Here are some inventions and innovations that scientists, inventors, and futurists have predicted, which may or may not come true!

2006 Tactile sensors comparable to human sensation

2007 Robotic space vehicles and facilities

2009 Fire-fighting robots that can find and rescue people

2010 Smart clothes that can alter their thermal properties

2011 House robots to fetch, carry, clean, and organize

2014 Nanorobots roaming in blood vessels

Predictions

2020 Artificial lungs, kidneys, and brain cells

2020 Cars that drive themselves on smart highways

2025 New forms of plants and animals from genetic engineering

2025 Extension of average life span to over 100 years

2025 Airplanes carrying passengers at 600 mph

2030 More robots than people in developed countries

2150 Average human life span may reach 200 years

Great Visionaries

Jules Verne, science fiction writer
This nineteenth-century writer Jules Verne wrote fantasy novels that included powered flight and journeys to the moon.

H.G. Wells, science fiction writer
He wrote a book in the 1890's about a time machine and time travel.

Sir Arthur C. Clarke, science fiction writer
He predicted the use of satellites. He also wrote about a computer with a mind of its own called HAL, an early example of artificial intelligence.

Buckminster Fuller, architect
He invented the geodesic dome and dreamed of floating cities connected by bridges to the mainland.

Areas to Watch

Nanotechnology: The use of extremely tiny (nano-sized) robots to carry out activities in medicine or in the environment.

Genetic engineering: Scientists are practicing techniques for moving genes from one plant or animal to another.

Artificial intelligence: Scientists and engineers all around the world are trying to build "smart" robots—robots that will be able to learn and think for themselves.

Read all about Luke and Sophie's unusual adventures in these great books!

1 Artrageous

2 Wonder Worlds

3 Wild Ideas

4 Look Out!

5 What's Next?

6 Game Plan

7 Gadget Hero

8 Bony Puzzle

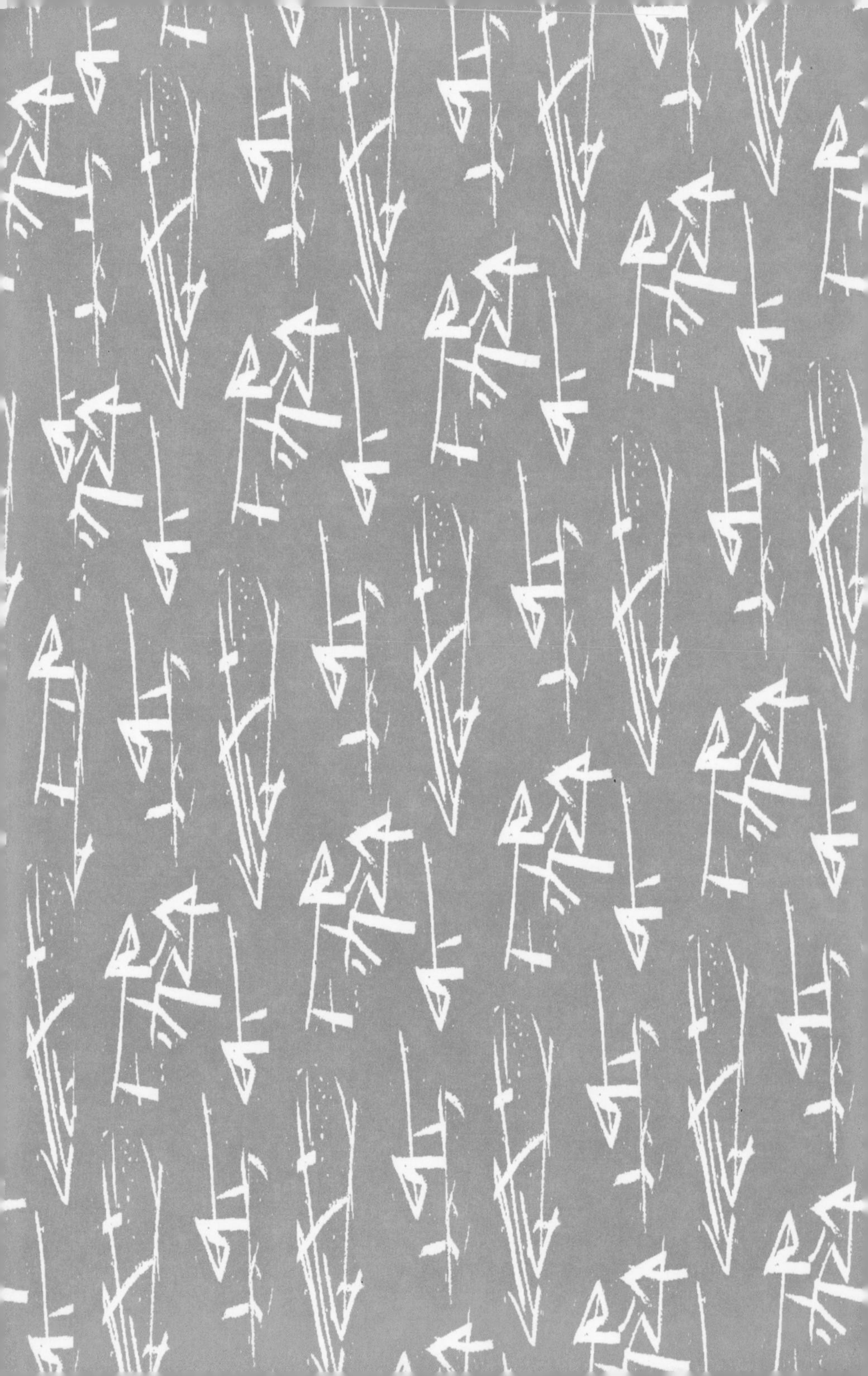